The Adventures of Eggnog the Bulldog: Meet Eggnog

Jennifer Berger

illustrated by Denise Prado

The Adventures of Eggnog the Bulldog: Meet Eggnog

This is a work of fiction.

Text copyrighted by Jennifer Berger ©2020

Illustrations copyrighted by A 2 Z Press LLC ©2020

Library of Congress Control Number: 2020907829

All rights reserved. No part of this book may be reproduced, transmitted, or stored in an information retrieval system in any form or by any means, graphic, electronic, or mechanical without prior written permission from the author and A 2 Z Press LLC.

Printed in the United States of America

A 2 Z Press LLC

PO Box 582

Deleon Springs, FL 32130

bestlittleonlinebookstore.com

sizemore3630@aol.com

440-241-3126

ISBN: 978-1-946908--19-3

Dedication

*In loving memory my brave and beautiful niece, Kelsey.
Thank you for showing me that there is hope in every sunrise and strength in every sunset.
You've taught me about the beauty of life, the importance of laughter, and the true meaning of unconditional love.
You will forever have my whole heart.*

This Book Belongs To

_____

Hello! My name is Eggnog!
Everyone says I am just too sweet to ignore,
Have you ever seen a bulldog as cute as me before?

I have extra big paws and a short, stubby tail,
My face is super wrinkly and I'm round like a whale!

I have big droopy jowls that hang from my lips,
My ears have small black spots that look just like chocolate chips!

My belly is pink and spotted,
kind of like a baby cow,

And I have a special brown mark that looks just like an eyebrow!

I live in Nogginland, which is every pup's dream come true,

Most dog houses are outside,
but mine is in my living room!

It has storage for my toys and lights that are bright pink!

It even has running water in case I'm thirsty and need a drink.

I have many nicknames - like Noggin and Noggy Bear,
Do you have any nickname you would like to share?

I'm an expert on sleeping and snacking on anything good,

And when I am not snoozing, I am looking for sticks out in the woods!

Every morning when I wake, I shake my jowls everywhere,
And sometimes when I shake, I send slobber flying through the air!

Mom laughs and makes my breakfast, she thinks I'm cute at least,
I sit just like a good girl as I patiently await my feast!

One, two, three ... I slurp my meal down just like that!
I hold the bulldog record for eating in seven seconds flat!

Next, I gulp down my water and spill it all over the floor,
I leave a trail of drool behind me as I head straight for the door!

When it is time for me go outside, I explore and have some fun,
I will search high and low for sticks until I find the perfect one!

I waddle over hills and under
each old fallen tree,
I circle round a large rock and
marvel at what I see.

I choose my favorite one and carefully pick it from the pile,

I proudly head back to my home with my stick and my smile.

I reach the front door of my home and look up at mom with pride,

She laughs and says, "Ok, Eggnog, you can bring that one inside."

I squeeze it through the door
and let out a little yawn,

What a big adventure mom and I just went on!

I carry my stick right to my bed, where I contemplate a snooze,
Maybe I'll just rest my eyes for a minute, or maybe two.

I snuggle up with my prize placed safely on the floor,

I think that when I wake, I will go out to hunt for more!

I let out a sleepy sigh and roll right on my bulldog back,

My work today is done, so I'll sleep ... 'til it's time for another snack.

Sweet, sweet dreams from Nogginland,

Where everything is grand!!

The End

***Jennifer Berger with Eggnog and Igloo*

Love is a seven letter word for Jen - Bulldog. The Berger's live in Dutchess County, New York. Jen has been sharing her beloved pets with others for years and now Eggnog is the star of a charming and delightful series of children's books!

Jen has always enjoyed reading 'The Berenstain Bears' books to her niece and nephew. They are especially memorable because Jen's own mom read them to her. She knows the value in reading to young children.

Jen loves fashion and travelling to Disney World and Italy. She enjoys photography and making others smile with a single snapshot!

Jen's passion is raising money for childhood cancer. She is genuinely kind to people and finds it amazing what the power of a hug can do.

She enjoys being outdoors and Fall is her favorite season Nothing compares to a hot apple cider donut on a crisp October day in New York.

She spends time with family and her two dogs, Eggnog and Igloo. Her favorite holiday is Christmas and why she named her girl, Eggnog. She even plays Christmas music in July!

Jen loves all dogs but will forever be a bulldog owner. They make her smile every day and apparently so many others too!

Eggnog

Eggnog is a four-year-old English Bulldog who has become a social media sensation with over a half a million followers across all of her social platforms. Living in what is affectionately referred to as "Nogginland," Eggnog loves donuts, hates the bath, and has named herself a certified stick saver, often bringing her beloved branches right inside the house! Her signature single brown eyebrow and unique spotted white fur, coupled with her cute Christmas name, makes Eggnog a precious pup that you surely will never forget! Her custom built dog house is what skyrocketed her to fame and is her favorite place to play! It is equipped with tunnels, toy storage, a ramp to the upper level and even running water! She's been featured by countless news channels, blogs, and media outlets and has become quite the viral sensation worldwide! Follow her real life adventures @eggnogthebulldog and enjoy the savory sweetness of Eggnog, all year round!

A2Z Press LLC

A2Z Press LLC published this work. A2Z Press LLC is a publishing company created by Terrie Sizemore for the purpose of publishing literary works by new and aspiring writers. All content is G-rated. We welcome your submissions of ideas for children's literature as well as adult and self-help topics. Science and medicine, holidays and other interesting topics are all welcome. Submit queries to sizemore3630@aol.com or PO Box 582 Deleon Springs, FL 32130

Visit our Website

Visit www.eggnogthebulldog.com to find out what Eggnog is up to now!

Other Books by A 2 Z Press Authors

Animal Academy

There is a Poem Inside of Me

How To Succeed In College

H is for Horse

The 23rd Psalm

D is for Dog

Golden Tales: Havoc in Rome

Chilly: The Lost Little Snowboy Ornament

Fairy Hairy Trouble

And More!

CPSIA information can be obtained
at www.ICGtesting.com
Printed in the USA
LVHW070758210820
663788LV00005B/46